Disclaimer

This is a work of fiction. Any names, businesses, characters, events, incidents and places are either the product of the author's imagination or used in a fictitious manner. Any resemblance to actual people, living or dead, or actual events or occurrences is purely coincidental.

Wizard's Quest

Spell Master
Book 1

By Blaine Hart
Copyright © 2016

Check Out all My Books and Audio Books at:
www.LordHartRules.com

Table of Contents

Chapter 1: Fools and Their Bodies are Soon Parted

The story I am about to tell you is from the beginning, but not from the start. Nor is this the end of the story. It is, never the less, an important point to begin the story of the mighty gnome sorcerer Vaskerath, who was birthed under the rare heavenly occurrence of fire. His control of magic and the beings of the astral plain of Hel would become legendary. Here is how it all began.

Far to the North, but not as far north as the frozen wastes, lay the Highlands, a land of ancient mountains and a maze of underground caverns which was inhabited by bears, trolls and other nasty creatures. The Highlands were not a particularly safe place for a gnome to spend his days. However, there was a treasure and power to be found here, and that was all Vaskerath needed to compel him to this most dangerous part of the realm. With his magically enslaved Imp's help, Vaskerath figured he could do the job fairly easily, get some treasure, and make an escape before the guild even became aware of what he was up to.

Vaskerath entered the simple looking tavern, knowing that this was where the thieves guild would be looking for him. It seemed to him at the time that the safest place for him to be was where his enemies expected him to be. Especially when they had something you wanted and were commissioned to obtain it.

The gnome made himself clearly visible to all in the 'The Unhappy Troll', drinking the warm tavern beer with seeming abandon. He was waiting for the Halfling from the Thieves' Guild to make an appearance. They were each looking for the other; advantage Vaskerath, as long as his Imp Devlin sticks to the plan, which he did do... *sometimes*.

In his first real taste of power as an apprentice, Vaskerath had somehow pulled the powerful Imp, Devlyn, from his home in the astral plain. (He had actually been trying to summon a fire demon, a talent well beyond his capacity as an apprentice.) The Imp, as a summoned creature, had become his slave. Just not always a dependable one.

Vaskerath recognized the halfling as soon as he came in the door a few minutes later. The Thieves Guild made no attempt to hide who they were. Few dared to stand in their way. This halfling carried himself with an aura of invincibility that made Vaskerath think, 'easy prey.'

The gnome spotted where Vaskerath sat, seemingly alone, and joined him at the table. "You have room for a fellow traveler here?" he asked the gnome.

"Of course, in a crowded tavern one must make room for new friends," Vaskerath said smiling.

"Perhaps a game of chance?" asked the halfling, "To make the evening go quicker."

"Why not," answered Vaskerath, as the halfling waved over the tavern master to bring them some fresh drinks.

The point in the evening when Vaskerath knew that he could no longer pay back his debts had come and gone, officially about two hours ago. Things had gotten so bad that even *he* knew that he was in big trouble. If he didn't turn up a king on his next card, then things were likely to get much worse... very quickly.

Things had gotten so bad that Vaskerath had forced himself to stop drinking the strong Bandy Bramble apple-scented liquor, even though it was the tavern master's specialty. He needed to think straight if he was going to get through this with his body intact, so, from here on out, beer only. And if he won, he'd drink the grog. That was fair.

The tavern master knew things could get nasty ever since he'd seen Vaskerath's opponent sharpening his blade beneath the table. And he was not sharpening it in an idle way, it looked like the little fellow meant business. He was *careful*, taking the time to work out knots in the steel, to really go over the whole blade with extra precision while he eyed Vaskerath carefully.

Vaskerath's opponent had known things were going good ever since the gnome had begun betting his own teeth. "How many does a mouth need, anyway?" the gnome grinned, revealing two crooked rows of shining teeth like little copper nuggets.

The gnome had at least fifty good teeth in his mouth and the Halfling felt his lips curl into a smile. Teeth fetched a high price with the hunters. Hunters liked to sharpen them up and use them for arrowheads. It was rumored that a gnomes tooth could cut right through a vampire's skin, like a hot knife through pudding. There were some hunters who even went so far as to collect enough teeth to forge tooth blades. The Halfling had himself never laid eyes on one of these famous blades.

In addition to every last coin in his traveler's chest, down to the coppers, Vaskerath's debts included twelve of his teeth and one of his big toes; the other toe was currently being wagered. This Halfling dealt in *toes*. Not a customer Vaskerath ever should have gamed with. The the situation was bad indeed.

"Call it," said the Halfling. His voice was ugly, croaking yet squeaky, like a troll pinching its nose. He hadn't started the game sounding like *that*. The Halfling had been well dressed, classy and polite. It had been the Halfling who'd invited *him* to the game, just a simple game for a few pints of Bandy Bramble. No big wagers. They were all friends here, all in good company.

"I'd *love* a pint," Vaskerath had said, confirming his thought of *easy prey,* after the Halfling let him win the first few games. *I've got you where I want you now.* Vaskerath thought. He'd hated Halflings for a long time, certainly long before they'd threatened to cut his toes off. He hated them partially because they did things like wear fancy silk waistcoats, and partially because they thought they were superior, and also because the smoke of their pipes was too fruity for his tastes. But mostly, he hated them because they were *taller* than he was.

"Three," Vaskerath said, smiling uneasily, showing his teeth. Might as well use them while he had them. "Three of Hearts."

"Three of Hearts," repeated the Halfling. He flipped his card, King of Diamonds. The Halfling put his knife on the table so loudly and heavily that the grog in its glass shook. It was a good knife. You couldn't find knives like that this far down south. It was made of strong, dark, northern steel; an inheritance, or a lucky bet. Vaskerath's eyes lit up with greed at the sight of it.

"That's both toes, gnome," the Halfling said. "You're running out of body."

"Yes, yes, running out of body. Yes, that's *funny*." Vaskerath laughed loudly. *You stupid Halfling I hope you get eaten by a dragon.* He thought.

"I'm afraid it's time to collect." He set the knife on the table. The dark heavy croak of the steel was terrible.

"Oh please!" Vaskerath clutched the table with both hands and leaned forward. "Just one, just one more *tiny little* bet! It's not my night, you understand. I swear, swear on the Nine Gods" (he crossed his hands over his chest and bowed piously) "on the Nine, I swear. Just *one more*." *I have you now, the map*, Vaskerath thought. It was time for the Imp to make his play.

"But my dear gnome," the Halfling laughed. "What else of you do I want? What else could I possibly need? I'm a simple Halfling; Porridge in the morning, pints in the evening, tea and tobacco in the afternoons."

Vaskerath supported his chin with a hand. He began to think. He strained himself with all his thinking. Then he noticed the Halfling's head, bald and shining like oil. "My scalp!" the gnome cried. "Surely a gentleman Halfling is in need of a good scalp?"

"A scalp?" The Halfling stroked his chin with his long nails.

"I've taken good care of it," Vaskerath said, eagerly grabbing a handful of his dark hair and giving it a tug to demonstrate.

"Yes, indeed," the Halfling had to admit. "A fine scalp,"

"It'll be leagues before you find another like it."

"Oh I don't doubt that," smiled the Halfling. His fingers ceased their movement. "But my dear fellow, you understand that I'm ..."

"You're *what*?" Vaskerath's elbows crashed down on the table, upsetting the silverware. The noise was loud, but the only ones to turn in their direction were the two hunters, warming their boots at the fireplace.

"Apprehensive."

"Apprehensive?"

"Apprehensive," the Halfling repeated.

It took Vaskerath a moment to find a response, and then his face split into a wide grin. "Really, you can't, you can't *possibly* think – not a gentleman Halfling like yourself! – why, we've become practically bosom brothers these past few hours."

"Oh, *yes*," the Halfling chuckled. "Yes, you're a fine fellow indeed. Absolute class." The chuckle dried. "But we Halflings are known for our caution. And imagine the shock, the indignation, the *betrayal* you'd feel in my shoes, if you discovered the next day that your reward was anything less than *authentic*."

"You don't think I would use a *re-growth spell on myself do you*?" Vaskerath's voice was a squeak filled with disappointed outrage. "Really, I can absolutely assure you that once a limb has left my body it stays gone for good. I'm no troll. My body wouldn't even think of regenerating anything new. On that... on that my lovely Halfling, I swear on the Nine (Vaskerath crossed his hands across his chest and bowed once more)."

"The Nine again?" the Halfling notched an eyebrow. "Really, with your luck I'd advise you to find some new gods. Or perhaps you could try the demons, if the gods are already taken. They're always recruiting new disciples, atleast that's what the hunters say."

Vaskerath shrugged in a helpless, what-can-you-do way.

"Very well," the Halfling considered. "Very...*well*. But you understand, I don't truly need a new scalp. At least not today. In fact, it's something I'd never even considered before. And then there's the matter of what to do with the old one? I really hate to be wasteful. No. The one I have is fine for now."

"One of my legs, maybe? I can get by with one. Or a whole hand? Just think what a gentleman Halfling could accomplish with *three hands*."

"No, no," the Halfling shook his head vigorously. "My dear fellow, now we're simply going backwards."

"Well... *well* there has to be..." Vaskerath was lost for words and couldn't complete the sentence.

"Let us consider," the Halfling put his hands together and made a steeple of fat, sausage-like fingers. "What is it that would truly interest me? What can you *offer*? Deals should be fair, simple and balanced, as I know you'll agree. Since I know what *you* want from *me*, I believe it's time that we consider the other side of the problem."

Vaskerath's eyes flashed to the far end of the table, where a satchel sat that contained a little wooden box. A quite ordinary little box, and completely nondescript, if you didn't count the circle branded on its cover. The contents of this box were so valuable that Vaskerath had been more than willing to sacrifice not only all his money, but some of his teeth and toes as well.

Just looking at the box made Vaskerath's hands sweat. He reached into the pockets of his tattered overcoat and wiped his hands busily on the crumpled piece paper they held. The Halfling frowned at him, wondering if he was trying to secretly cast a spell. Vaskerath grinned and held the corner of the paper to demonstrate its innocence.

"Very well," the Halfling said gravely. "This is quite enough fooling around, I think."

"Fooling around?" Vaskerath was alarmed. "This is a d-d-discussion we're having, yes?"

The Halfling collapsed his steeple of fingers into two small fists. His eyes became small and narrowed, and shifted from Vaskerath to the knife. Then he sighed, picked the knife up and began testing the edge absentmindedly. He did not smile.

"Vaskerath," the tone was serious, businesslike. "I'm sure you'd like this to be done with as quickly as I, so let me be brief. I am on a deadline, that is, I have until, yes, until *exactly tonight to complete my assignment.*"

Vaskerath's hands wrung the paper into a wet little ball. He mumbled incoherently to himself. He couldn't recall telling the Halfling his name.

"I have until tonight to collect what I've come here for," the Halfling's eyes rose to meet his. Calm and sharp as northern steel. Vaskerath's throat swallowed nervously and panic was starting to creep into his mind. *It can't end like this.* He thought. "Maybe you can guess what it is that I need? The Halfling asked menacingly, his eyes locked on Vaskerath's own."

The knifepoint was directed at his chest. Centimeter by centimeter it rose, reached his throat, rose higher, then stopped at his forehead.

"You little bastard!" Vaskerath nearly leapt from his chair but the knife's steady point kept him still, as he looked around wildly. No one else was watching the scene. The tavern master was pouring Bandy. The lyrist was strumming in the corner by the fire to an audience of Halflings and off-duty hunters. Some of them were singing, their voices hearty and confident with liquor. What he wouldn't have given to be able to join them! To be able to enjoy just one more glass of Brandy, to be out of this terrible *mess*!

"Don't make a scene," the Halfling cautioned, "or I'll flay you right here and now. Surely, Vaskerath, you must have known this day was coming. You committed the crime. You ought to expect punishment."

"But there was nothing there!" Vaskerath protested. He'd guessed who the Halfling meant immediately. "I mean, what I mean to say is that, is that he, your friend Davenport…"

"*Guild Master* Davenport," the Halfling hissed, scowling furiously, "is nobody's *friend.*"

"I only won a few coppers. There was nothing more. *Nothing*. He'd already fenced it using a concealing Spell. I swear… I absolutely *swear on…*"

The Halfling moved the knife to the bulging artery in Vaskerath's neck. "You stole from the *Guild Master* of *Thieves*; you foolish gnome. The Master has ordered burnings for offences less than a few coppers. You're lucky to be getting off light as you are."

The Halfling glowered. "Even if it was nothing more than *a few coppers.*"

The paper Vaskerath wiped his hands on had become soggy. "So… so," he tried to say, but the words failed him. "That's everything? Farewell to the world and all that? There's not a chance, not even the tiniest, little piece of hope for a deal?"

"Afraid not," the Halfling said. The empathy in his voice almost sounded real. Touching. "You'll get one more draw, just so everything appears fair. You'll need a Queen or higher, but it'll be the Nine of Spades." Vaskerath looked shocked. "Don't act so surprised, we're thieves. You wouldn't catch one of us playing a game that wasn't rigged. After you've lost we'll step outside, I'll cut your throat nice and clean, and that'll be the end of it. You get to keep your toes after all."

"And what about my teeth?"

The knife flashed, pointing towards the deck of cards. "It's time." Vaskerath withdrew the soggy paper from his pocket and placed his trembling hand over the deck, but did not draw.

"But you haven't given me your word."

The Halfling frowned. "On what?"

"The map," his eyes flashed to the satchel. "If I win, I get the map."

"But you won't win."

"Then it's safe for you to give me your word. There is the expression 'honor among thieves?' I hope that remains true with you"

"Well," said the Halfling. "*Well*, I am a master thief." he lowered his knife, and stretched out his hand. Vaskerath took the pudgy hand and shook it with conviction.

"And now it's time," the Halfling said, stretching out his slightly crumpled fingers before they rested again menacingly on the dagger.

"I suppose we'd better get down to it," Vaskerath nodded. The cards were warm beneath his hand. His fingers slid over the surface, traced the complex outline of the paper. "Blessed be the Nine," he mumbled as he drew. "Blessed be the Nine..."

"*The Nine have blessed you indeed,*" a voice whispered back in his ear. Vaskerath looked at his card.

Well, it certainly took them long enough. He reached across the table, threw down the King, and then filled his mouth with the Halfling's grog as the thief sat there dumbfounded.

Chapter 2: The Scribe

"You *scummy*... you *little*... you cheap *filthy gnome!*" But by the time the Halfling had recovered from the shock of seeing the King of Hearts, Vaskerath had looped the satchel over his shoulder and was stumbling out of his seat.

"That's *miiine!*" the Halfling screamed as he lunged across the table and caught Vaskerath by the frayed end of his overcoat. Vaskerath whirled around. "You gave your word!" he tried to say, but he'd forgotten about the grog — un-swallowed, filling his cheeks! — and instead of words, his mouth instead ejected a long, slimy-greenish stream of liquid grog that flew all over the enraged thief's face.

The Halfling fell back, wiping his eyes. And then something very strange happened. The glass of grog on the table rocked and rose into the air, unsupported by neither hand nor string. It hovered there for a moment, several feel above the table, and then came crashing down with a deafening shatter on the Halfling's head. The glass and the grog created a miniature explosion. The Halfling slumped to the ground and did not follow Vaskerath out the door.

For a pudgy little creature less than three feet tall, the gnome could run surprisingly quick. In a matter of just a few minutes he was at the bridge and over the river that marked the official entrance into town. He then paused to catch his breath.

"What took you so *long*?" he wheezed into the open air. "I feel like I've lost twenty years off my life waiting for you."

"*The master says 'come' and we come,*" a voice answered him back. "*The master said nothing about when and how we should come.*"

"And I suppose you can't be expected to use common sense, either?" Vaskerath huffed angrily.

"*The master says 'use common sense' and we use common sense. But the master didn't say this.*"

"This is strange," Vaskerath said as he frowned at the blankness in front of him. He'd never been in the habit of talking to himself, and doing so now gave him a wormy, uncomfortable sensation, like a bad-fitting shirt or a pebble in his boot. "Do you have any idea how long the Concealment Spell will last? I don't want to have to talk to the thin air for the rest of the night. It's...*creepy.*"

"*The master knows his incantations better than I. It is for him to know and for me to act. I am sorry I can do no more.*"

"Oh, you've done enough already," Vaskerath said, none too friendly. "But don't go running off to I-don't-know-where. Don't even think about it. I need you here with me. We're still a long ways from safety and the Thieves guild is a dangerous foe to cross."

"Whatever the master orders."

"You're exactly right." Vaskerath replied. "You should try and be smarter about my orders you little devil. Your little games grow wearisome! If you weren't so valuable... well... I'd teach you a binding lesson you'd never forget!" Vaskerath was fuming now, but he knew it was futile. They had gone through this routine before... it seemed like a hundred times.

Calming himself, Vaskerath quickly crossed over the bridge and headed up the path to the right that went over a small hill covered in plants and trees. The landscape was picturesque; with cute little houses leaking smoke from their chimneys and the sun reflecting nicely off the stream below. All of it worked together to give the place an hospitable aura that has served the town well over the years. A place of easy-living, of fresh pints of ale and slabs of meat dripping juice over an inviting fire. A place where fat little Halflings drank themselves to sleep and where old hunters congregated to spend whatever coin they'd managed to collect from lands near and far. A place of slack purses and easy minds.

It was supposed to be *simple*, thought Vaskerath. A few card games, a few tricks from his familiar, and soon he'd be rolling around in his winnings. It should have been simple. He wasn't supposed to have accidentally stolen from the *Guild Master of Thieves;* wasn't supposed to have lifted coin off of the Most Powerful Underworld Boss in the country; he wasn't supposed to have ended up like a rat fleeing a burning barn. It was supposed to have gone *different*.

Life was difficult enough for a poor gnome in a foreign land. Coin wasn't exactly in plenty and friends were difficult to find. In fact, apart from his impish companion Devlyn and the drinking companions he'd found at the tavern, the gnome had kept almost entirely to himself. He spent most of his days listening to the lyrists, watching the swans on the river, or practicing from the slim book of elementary-grade incantations he'd pinched off a drunk mage.

Six weeks he'd stewed here and what did he have to show for it? All he had was the contents in that satchel... and it better be what he thought it was. Otherwise he was seriously considering binding his imp to the bottom of the ocean for a century and then ending it all. But no... he couldn't do that. Not with so much magic out there. His mouth began to water at just the thought of it. He once again looked at his beautiful surroundings and shook himself out of it. He had learned a cool spell that allowed him to cover distance like a horse for about three minutes. And on his good days, he was able to snap his fingers and light his pipe without matches or a candle. Not to mention that just a few hours ago he'd cast his first ever concealment spell, although it wasn't so much actual conjuration as it was rubbing his hands on an old scrap of parchment and muttering some words. Still, it had worked. Devlyn was invisible. His progress was coming along. But at this rate he'd be a century old by the time he was able to cast anything of serious use.

Vaskerath's pudgy little legs carried him past the hill and over to the town inn. It was a cheap, ugly public house that resembled a leaning stack of pancakes. The clientele was mostly other gnomes like him, along with a few deadbeat Halflings, and of course, the Scribe. Vaskerath's heartbeat quickened at the prospect of meeting with the shadowy figure as he clutched the satchel closely to his chest.

"You haven't been up to any trouble at the taverns, have ye?" inquired the fat innkeeper, casting a glance at the out-of-breath Vaskerath.

"Not any more than some," the gnome grinned, glad that he still had all his teeth. He didn't like the challenge in the innkeeper's eyes one bit. "Our mutual friend..." Vaskerath began but the innkeeper interrupted.

"Same place as always. Corner. Smoking that long pipe of his."

"Many thanks," Vaskerath mumbled and hurried over to the common room, which at this hour of the night, was dense with a crowd similar to that of the tavern he was just at.

"You'll stay right here next to me, understand?" Vaskerath hissed to the empty space at his side.

Devlyn's silvery voice responded. *"I wouldn't dream of leaving the master's side."*

"Smart imp." Vaskerath flashed his teeth, all fifty of them.

The Scribe sat at a corner table. His body was covered in long black robes and his hands where covered in black gloves. He wore a long cowl that shielded his eyes and nose and left only his mouth uncovered, through which protruded the stem of his pipe. It was indeed a long pipe, just as the innkeeper had described. Like a bramble branch grown by neglect. The scribe inhaled deeply from his pipe and blew out a large plume of white smoke. The tobacco made Vaskerath cough.

"You're late." The Scribe's voice was baritone and slightly louder than a whisper. For an answer, Vaskerath shrugged and pulled out the stool from under the table. The Scribe lifted his legs and placed them on the stool, indicating that he was not allowing Vaskerath to sit.

"It took longer than expected."

"You're unreliable, gnome."

"I got the prize," Vaskerath said sharply, drawing the box out of the satchel. He would prefer to get this interview over and done with as soon as he could. He didn't like this Scribe one bit. Not the bleeding pipe, nor his voice, nor the curt and forceful manner he had, as if he was so superior to gnomish scum like him. He was just like the detested mages with whom he had spent a brief time at the academy with to learn his first magical incantations; just like spell-Master Lukas and all his cronies.

But Vaskerath especially didn't like the feeling that he was being analyzed, even if the Scribe's eyes were completely covered.

"Open it," the Scribe commanded.

"No key." Vaskerath replied with a shrug.

"You're a conjurer, aren't you? Don't tell me you haven't learned how to open a simple lock yet?"

"Wouldn't want to risk damaging anything." Vaskerath tried to sound confident. He directed his train of vision straight at the area where the Scribe's eyes should be and stared. He had the feeling that the Scribe was staring right back at him and even into him. Vaskerath shuddered.

"Very well," said the Scribe at last and placed a gloved hand on the box. Vaskerath tried to catch what he whispered, but it was too soft and sounded as if it was spoken in a foreign language. He watched as the Scribe's hand came away. The little circle on the box began to glow, red, then blue, before finally settling into a dull grey. The insignia filled in completely with what looked like black ink. The box sprang open. Inside rested a curled leaf of paper, burnt at the edges.

"A novice lock. Those thieves don't know anything about protecting their property." The scribe laughed and haughtily.

"So it's all there? No damage? No problem?" Vaskerath asked. H reached out to grab the paper but the Scribe slapped it away with surprisingly quick reflexes and a hiss of disapproval.

"Oh, very well." Vaskerath checked first one pocket of his coat, then the other; then the front pockets of his trousers, then the back.

"The master put the money in the satchel, if he will remember."

Hurriedly Vaskerath dug down into the satchel and retrieved the leather purse he'd been searching for. He placed it on the table between them. The Scribe opened the pouch and counted the money. Vaskerath wrung his hands.

"Very well." The Scribe said. Delicately, as if he were handling a dragon egg, the Scribe lifted the parchment and set it on the table. He put his hands in the air over it and then drew them apart. The paper unrolled. It was blank.

"You must know, gnome, I can detect at once if you are trying to deceive me in any way. And should that be the case," the Scribe left the rest of the sentence incomplete, letting Vaskerath's imagination fill in the details.

"Wouldn't dream of it," the gnome said hastily. He wished this fellow would finish already. The waiting was killing him. And he didn't like that the Scribe seemed to be addressing both him *and* the thin air beside him, as if he *knew* Vaskerath wasn't alone. "I can't even pick a lock. How would I be able to deceive a someone as powerful as you?"

It was a feeble answer but it did the trick. The Scribe murmured "very well" once more and turned his attention back to the paper. Then, as if he were untying an invisible knot, he began to move his hands over the map. Vaskerath couldn't have replicated or even described the complex process. To him, it appeared like a lot of mumbo-jumbo, a lot of senseless hand gestures that he half thought were the Scribe's way of confusing him so that he wouldn't be able to understand the actual process of what was really going on.

And at first, nothing seemed to be going on. Then, little by little, dark splotches appeared on the paper. Like fresh stains, they grew bolder, more clear. After a few minutes, Vaskerath was able to make out the shapes of trees and of rivers, and the little dumpling turrets of the hill-lands. Finally, cutting through it all, the string of a pathway appeared, curling around hillock and along river, and then leaving a large splotch in the same shape as the seal on the box at the base of a mountain —Garom's Gorge! — Vaskerath knew. Not that he'd ever been to the mountain himself, but he'd seen it on other maps. It was about a day's hike from the hill country.

The map finished materializing. "That's it, then?" Vaskerath felt the breath escape that he'd been holding in. "It doesn't say what's there or maybe even *who's* there or, well, anything *useful*?"

"Everything, yes," the Scribe folded his hands carefully in his lap. A cloud of pipe smoke rose. "Everything is shown that I can draw from this map."

"From this map? You mean there's more?"

"At least one more. A sister. Surely even you can see that this map's not complete?"

Vaskerath squinted, trying to get a reading. Sure enough, in the upper right hand corner of the map, at the splotch at the base of the mountain, the path cut off like an interrupted sentence.

"Whatever the thieves have hidden, you won't find it here. You'll need to find the other half."

Vaskerath quivered in rage. Then calmed himself. "At Garom's Gorge?" He was liking this less and less with every minute. Why would a bunch of thieves need to hide anything so far away? Wasn't the hill country good enough to keep their stolen goods? How did he know this wasn't a ruse and that he might not even find anything so far into the wild? And Garom's Gorge…wasn't there rumored to be, well, it was in a forest, and the Nine only knew *what* he might find there. What if the rumors where true?

But Vaskerath was not well suited to consider 'what ifs' for too long. All that mattered was that there was long lost magic power to be attained! Suddenly there was a clamor in the entrance hall along with the sounds of many tramping feet, and of knives being quickly drawn, and then one voice in particular cut through the inn… the nasally, harsh voice of a vengeful Halfling out for blood.

"Scribe!" Vaskerath cried, whirling back to face his mysterious companion, though he was already too late. The Scribe had vanished.

"Vaskerath!" the Halfling cried in a bloodthirsty scream. "I'll have your head, you cheating gnome!"

Quick as he could, the gnome stuffed the map and box into the satchel and dashed towards the back exit. Luckily the Scribe loved to sit near the back, and from the sounds of things, he hadn't yet been spotted, although no doubt the innkeeper had already ratted him out.

"The master doesn't want to gather any supplies for the journey?" Devlyn whispered in his head.

"Supplies? Are you out of your mind!" he shouted. "We'll get to keep our heads if we're lucky!"

The back door wasn't bolted. A stroke of luck, Vaskerath crossed his arms and bowed his head as he ran out the door. If the Nine ever *did* bother to lend him a hand, he wanted to make sure he had good credit in the piety department.

The inn was situated against a hill behind which stretched the first few trees of the Long Wood. No doubt the thieves would search there for him, but even if the woods weren't really all that *thick,* it wouldn't be easy-going, certainly not in the nighttime. He could probably hide out pretty easily until morning. And then there was a whole host of new problems to look forward to, because if the thieves didn't flay him alive, he could starve, or fall into a gulch and break his little gnome neck, or drown in a swamp, or …

"The master is absolutely, positively sure he doesn't want to gather any supplies for the journey?"

That stupid Imp! Vaskerath, harried as he was, mentally reminded himself to give the creature a good thrashing when they were safe in the woods, visible or not.

"Have I not already told you?" Vaskerath hissed.

So focused was he on abusing the invisible Imp, Vaskerath lost focus, and in another two steps and he'd have been directly under the powerful hooves of one of the enormous Northern ponies this region was famous for, three of which were tied to the post next to the inn. He gave a little squeal and leapt back.

"Why didn't you warn me!" he cried.

"But I already asked the master if he was absolutely, positively sure he didn't want to gather any supplies?"

Only then did Vaskerath notice the saddlebags. No doubt the horses belonged to the thieves. Vaskerath couldn't recall having seen them when he got to the public house. And they must have anticipated a long journey, as the bags were brimming with fruit, loaves of bread and dried meat.

"Quick!" he said, "give me a boost!"

Vaskerath slung the satchel around his shoulder and gripped the saddle straps and tried to mount the nearest giant horse. The distance was too great and he fell on the ground.

"I said give me a boost!"

"With respect to the master," said the Imp, *"one mount won't solve our problem."*

One mount? What did this Imp mean? Vaskerath thought. Suddenly, an idea hit him. He gave up trying to mount and approached the other two mounts, his hands rubbing furiously. From around the corner came the sound of voices, the Halfling's squeak dominating over all.

Vaskerath had never attempted to use his fire spell on anything more than his pipe or to cook a few rabbits. Now, if he wanted to keep his body in one piece, he'd need to do more than he'd ever done in the past, and he had only one shot at it.

Careful to avoid the hind legs, he maneuvered himself until he was below the horse's belly, continuously rubbing his hands. A telltale red spark like a ruby began to materialize. Vaskerath slowed his breath and ignored the sound of the approaching thieves. He was finding the Path, directing his energy, and he felt it expand in his hands, it became something more than a spark.

"There he is!" the Halfling shouted. "By the Nine, what's he *doing*?"

And then all of a sudden, Vaskerath felt his Energy open completely. *"O-goyn!"* he shouted, using the Ancient Tongue. A tongue of red flame appeared, hovering, incandescent over his open palm. It wavered for a split second and then attacked the pony's tender underside.

By the time the creature was really thrashing, Vaskerath was safely out from underneath. A word to the Imp and he was rising, lifted by an invisible force onto the back of the third powerful horse.

"The horses! He's attacking the horses!"

The thieves were visible now. There was the Halfling, his waistcoat blotted with bloodstains, with a tall man that Vaskerath didn't recognize, and finally, Guild Master Davenport himself, with his silver hair whipping around his shoulders like a wolf's tail, crossbow at the side which he quickly hefted to fit a bolt.

It had only been a singe, but the other two horses were wailing and thrashing about in fits, straining their ropes. Vaskerath, flame still in hand, directed its tongue towards the rope securing his own beast, and when it snapped, he quickly brought it down on his own horses' flanks.

"Hold on tight!" Vaskerath shouted to his Imp as the horse leapt up on two legs, startled by the pain. He felt a crossbow bolt whiz by his ear, missing him by inches.

Davenport was loading another bolt, but by the time he fit it into the weapon, it was too late. The second the horses' feet had come back to the earth, it had shot off like a startled bird with Vaskerath holding on for dear life. The only sign that he had ever been there was the horse's hoof prints in the muddy ground.

Chapter 3: Through the Highlands

Vaskerath had dealt with horses exactly twice in his life. The first time when he'd been a lad, a few hairs shorter than he was today, and he had tried to feed the beast an apple. The horse had rejected the apple and took a sampling of his little finger instead, munching a nasty gash in it like it was a carrot. Vaskerath had vowed, (on the Nine), never to go within fifty leagues of one the filthy beasts again for as long as he lived. But life had a funny way of making him go back on his vows, and a few years after later he found himself in a similar position, sitting bare-back on a beautiful white mare he'd been told was "sweeter n' Hollybrune berries." But be that as it may, it didn't take the 'sweet thing' a long time to get tired of him, and before he knew it, he'd been laid flat on his back with the breath knocked out of him.

Both of those occasions flew through his mind as he flew through the forest on the back of the fire-startled horse. Vaskerath held on for dear life and this was doubtlessly the most terrifying thing he'd ever experienced. Not only because of the horse, a frightened and powerful muscle machine twenty times his size and capable of crushing him with one smartly placed hoof, but because he didn't have the slightest idea of *where he was going and what the thieves guild would do to him if they ever caught him.* The forest was fairly dense and suffocating like a wet quilt.

Finally, when he had the opportunity to tear himself away from the one thought running through his mind, *I'm going to die, I'm going to die, I'm going to die,* and focus on something different, he noticed things like the stars filtering in through the webby canopy above and the harmonies created by the interlacing voices of frogs and insects.

Little reminders, that indeed, he was still alive; neither captured by thieves nor murdered by horses. He realized that if he kept his wits about him, he just might live another day. If he could just get some more powerful magic... he could solve all his problems. And then, his thoughts where interrupted by a sharp slap in the face from a low-hanging branch. He rubbed his stinging cheek and forced himself to concentrate on staying on the horse.

So the mad ride continued, although for exactly how long Vaskerath couldn't say. He couldn't reach his pocket watch or see the horizon, so his guess was based on the facts that his hands were cold and stiff as icicles and his thighs had all but turned to pudding.

"With respect to the master, maybe it's time we stopped for the night?" Devlyn whispered.

Vaskerath almost leapt out of the saddle when he heard the voice. He'd forgotten all about the Imp.

"Stop?" he nearly cried, although his voice was hoarse from shouting and he couldn't manage anything more than a squeak. "You can stop us? Why have you waited until now to say anything? Stop us!" he tried not to make it sound as though he was pleading. *He* was the master, after all. Not the Imp.

There was no answer from the creature. All of a sudden, Vaskerath felt something like two hands push up against his back. Briefly he wondered if the Imp was trying to sabotage him by wrestling him out of the saddle. He began calling down all the most impressive, most gruesome, and most painful curses he could think of.

And then, as abruptly as it had begun, the wild ride ceased. The horse gave a whinny of protest, skidded to a stop, and began kicking up its front two legs high into the air, bending its back down and trying to throw off the two creatures weighing it down. Vaskerath had been able to keep himself on for so long through the adrenaline and the threat of losing his life. However, after such a long time and with his energy gone, this was the final straw. His thighs melted away from their clutch like butter in a pan. His hands became loose and watery, the muscles strained to their breaking point and beyond, and he plopped onto the ground with a little squelch.

By the time he picked himself up, there was nothing left of the horse but the sound of muffled hoof beats and broken branches.

"Sve'ti," Vaskerath raised an arm and let the spell illuminate the swampy darkness. Nothing to be seen but trees and a stream. And of course, now that the concealment spell had worn off, there was Devlyn.

The Imp had skin the color of charcoal and a head like a spoiled onion, with just a few white hairs sticking out. He wore sackcloth overalls, which he told Vaskerath he preferred to anything else, but at this moment, the clothing was stretched over the Imp like a handkerchief stretched over a drum.

So that's how he managed to stop the horse. He made himself too fat to carry. Usually thin as a sapling, the Imp had swollen himself to seven times his normal weight. Doughy clumps of fat covered his body. His neck was as thick as a bull's neck, and although his face was relatively unchanged, there was the same razor thin slice of a mouth, the same large, hooked nose, and the same set of tiny black eyes set too close together.

"Whatever the master orders," the imp said tauntingly, giving him a stupid smile.

"Well Devlyn, *well.*" Vaskerath grinned, trying to fit into that grin all the curses and abuses he'd never had the time in reality to say. "Well, you've really done it now. Beautiful work. Couldn't have picked a better spot myself, and that's for certain. But would you tell me, *please*, where exactly do you expect us to go, now that we're stuck in the middle of the forest? Not to mention the fact that you weigh enough to break the back of a fully grown northern pony." His grin disappeared. "Do you have any ideas?"

The Imp did not waver, though his face remained the same.

"Nothing?" Vaskerath repeated threateningly. "Not the tiniest, little thing? You know what my binding spell is going to do to you if something unfortunate like that should happen!"

"Whatever the master…"

"Whatever the master orders," Vaskerath finished. "You're exactly right, you little troll snot. I'll go ahead and let you think about that for a little while. No, no afraid not," he shook his head, smiling. "I don't think I'm going to redact your fat belly. Maybe after a night here alone in the wild you will think again before stranding us again in the wilderness like this!"

Without another word, Vaskerath spun on his heels and marched in the opposite direction. Devlyn's voice, weak and blubbery through his fat lips, said the word 'master please', but Vaskerath didn't pay it any attention. A few hours alone in the dark would do the Imp good, he reasoned. He needed to discipline the creature somehow, especially given all the close calls he'd experienced this day.

The Imp was over-confident. It seemed he'd forgotten that it was *he* who held the power; it was he who'd summoned the Imp; he who controlled their mutual fates; and only he who had the power to set Devlyn free or condemn him to a near eternity of suffering.

It had been five years since he had cast that summoning spell on that fateful day. An absolute novice he'd been, barely able to read the ancient texts, but convinced already that he knew everything there was to know about summoning, about conjuration. So one night, feeling especially self-assured after a few pints, he'd decided to give himself a little test. He was going to summon a *Fire Demon*. Sure, he'd been seriously practicing for only a couple years and all the masters had said that it takes no fewer than ten years before an aspirant can expect to have any luck summoning, but he just *knew* it was his night for success. He could feel it in hid gut.

And really, how hard could it be? He'd seen a master perform a conjuration before and there was nothing to it; you read from a book, waved your arms, made an Invitation (Vaskerath had heard something like, 'denizen of Hel, come forth', although he was pretty sure he could say whatever he wanted) and then boom bam boom, his very own *Fire Demon* to command at will.

If he considered things from a technical point of view, Vaskerath had indeed been far more successful than he or anyone else could have expected. He raised a spirit. That was at least apprentice-level conjuration, and even then the apprentices often have difficulties. Vaskerath had done it on his first try. He had opened the ancient book, waved his hands, and muttered a few incomprehensible words while making his Invitation, and in a ball of greasy orange fire he'd been welcomed by the ugly, sack-cloth wearing, pinched-face little Imp, Devlyn. *"Whatever the master orders."*

Vaskerath had wept like a new mother.

How much things had changed! How he'd come to despise the pathetic creature in just five years. How often he'd wished that he'd never been so foolish. So maybe that's why all the mages, without exception, agree that conjurations should be reserved for only the upper apprentices and the masters. Not because the spells are difficult, but because they are pretty much *irreversible*.

Of course, Vaskerath could free the Imp any time he wanted, or so the Ancient Texts made clear. What was less clear was how exactly he was supposed to do this. No book specified the particular words or motions he had to make. It was like he was just supposed to know. But of course, he'd never admitted this to Devlyn. The Nine only knew what the Imp might do if it knew that Vaskerath was powerless to set him free.

Vaskerath held out his glowing hands and risked a little more illumination. He was still deep in the forest, but a little ways away he could make out the dark, rain-streaked wall of a cliff. And where there were cliffs, there might be caves, and if there was a cave, then he wouldn't have to spend the night in the forest. Now that *would* be a stroke of luck. He raced forward.

He came steadily nearer the cliff wall, illuminating it part by part until all was at last visible. The stone was old, weathered and moss-eaten, and a clump of stones at the base gave notice that part of the cliff must have collapsed at one time. Behind the clumps of stone, with a bit of straining, he could just make out a small pocket carved into the stone.

The stones provided a natural barrier to the cave so that there was no danger of rainwater seeping in. It was cozy, dry, untouched, and all for him.

He put the satchel in the corner and lit a small fire using the dried leaves collected from the corners. Magic, even simple illumination spells, cost him energy, which he was now in dangerously short supply of. Better to do things the old fashioned way.

His fire blazing cheerfully, Vaskerath lit his pipe and thought of the Imp, cold, wet, fat and defenseless, to take his mind off his growling stomach. Five years ago he'd have felt bad for the creature. Five years ago they'd been the best of friends. Now, after so much time spent tethered to the disgusting creature, after having his grog spoilt by subtly placed toad guts and his arse singed by unseen embers, from near misses and close calls, he was content to let the creature suffer the night alone. And besides, maybe all that rainwater would act another wonder on the Imp's *smell*. Just thinking of it made Vaskerath shudder.

He wrinkled his nose, and tried to ignore the second growl of his stomach.

In the distance he thought he heard some distant thunder, or maybe it was the old cavern walls settling. At any rate, at any rate...

At any rate it wasn't Vaskerath's fate that afternoon or that night to enjoy his pipe or his fire, or even his fond memories. Because as he now knew, the noise hadn't come from him, but from the corner where a burly shadow like lay. Like a wizened old tree, the noise slowly began to enlarge, unfold, and to creep out of its corner pocket until it grew as tall as three gnomes stacked shoulder on shoulder. It's slow head swiveled to face the intruder, and its mouth, bearded by a wreath of tawny, mossy hair, opened like a furnace. There were more teeth in that mouth than Vaskerath could ever have lost playing cards.

Chapter 4: Into the Abyss

As Vaskerath shown his light into the darkness, he noticed that it was a Troll. A full-grown, cliff-dwelling, meat-chewing, bone-crunching, foul-smelling, angry mountain *troll*. Vaskerath nearly swallowed his tongue. Never mind the Thieves Guild. Never mind the Guild master Davenport or his sadistic Halflings. He'd be down on his knees kissing toes if he thought for a moment it'd get him out of this in one piece.

A tongue like a steak slapped the webbed mouth of the troll and licked a bit of what looked like blood from its lower lip. Then, like a rabbit going back into its den, the sound retreated into the mouth of the cave. Heavy grunts, followed by powerful bursts of putrid nostril air, were exhaled.

It was asleep.

It took Vaskerath a few seconds to consider the fact that he was still alive. He'd been so sure when he first saw the troll's open mouth he was done for. He couldn't move a muscle, even though he could clearly hear the troll's snores. Then, all of a sudden, came the realization that he needed to do something, that he needed to get himself out of this situation while he still had a chance to. It filled him with a kind of electricity.

His hands twitched and his feet slowly carried him towards the direction of the cave entrance.

"*Easy easy easy easy,*" he whispered to himself in his head. Troll grunts filled the chamber. The tongue protruded once more and slapped at a fly near the left nostril.

Vaskerath made turtle progress towards the cave entrance, inch by inch. It didn't feel like he was going anywhere, but eventually he was able to feel the coolness of the rain and the wind on his skin. And once he was just a bit closer, there'd be only the rocks that he'd have to pass over, and then he would be safe, free, back in the rain, but well, *there were worse things...*

It didn't take much longer for Vaskerath to realize what one of those worse things was. He'd been so occupied in edging out of the cave, on watching the troll for any signs of wakefulness, on minimizing his own noise to the nothingness of a rat scratching sand, that he'd either failed to notice his surroundings or his surroundings failed to notice the danger he was in. He was nearly out into the night, nearly free, but at that moment a stone came dislodged, whether from his movement or from the natural setting of the rocks, he did not know. And not just a little pebble, but a miniature boulder in its own right, the size of Vaskerath's head.

Clunk.

Clunk.

CLUUUUUUNNNK.

The stone came bounding down the jagged staircase of rocks leading towards the cave entrance, bouncing like what was soon to be his own head torn up from its roots. Sliding down past Vaskerath, it rolled to rest against the troll's nose.

Not a stir.

Vaskerath felt his breath drain out of him. Twice in one day he'd come a hair's breathe from certain death, only to be saved by some inexplicable miracle at the last minute. He crossed himself and bowed, and it was another stroke of luck that he'd chosen that particular moment to bend.

Directly overhead a second boulder as large as him came rolling down, crashing into Vaskerath's forgotten fire. The chamber was illuminated by showers of dancing sparks, scattering like the streamers of fireworks across the ground and walls with an ethereal and elusive beauty, as if the cavern were filled with shooting stars. Falling and dissipating across the grime-stained walls and into the empty, black recesses in the far corner, and across the brow of the sleeping troll.

The troll's nose twitched and the beast grunted. In the quickly falling blackness, Vaskerath watched with mounting horror as first one and then both putrid, yellow eyes became unglued, betraying their fearful glint. Their gaze fixed directly on him.

With a cry, Vaskerath flew up the stones and began to climb, dislodging boulders, rocks, and sand behind him. Stones whizzed down from high up above. Some of the smaller ones pelted him directly, though he hadn't yet been struck by anything bigger.

He thought he'd had a pretty good lead on the troll. The sound of quick, heavy breaths behind him made him think otherwise, maybe just a few more seconds. Just a handful and then the troll would tear him down from his perch, smash his skull, and probably devour him in one giant gulp. Wouldn't *that* make the thieves angry! Prey and treasure gone in one fell swoop. No chance for revenge, no chance to recover what they'd lost. Devoured by a hungry troll.

Vaskerath tried to laugh. If this was indeed the end, he didn't want to be too serious or fateful about it. Go out with a smile on the lips. There were worse things.

More rocks came pounding by. He heard the muffled punch of a stone on troll body, followed by an angry roar. The cave had scored a hit. Nature was on Vaskerath's side at least. But there wasn't much you could do against a mountain troll. The beasts were practically invincible. Growths were the vulgar word for them: cut off an arm or a toe or a head and it made no difference, they just grew it right back like hair. What could a few stones possibly do to him? What was the use in trying to get out when the beast would wind up hunting him down anyway?

"Master!"

Vaskerath felt his ears twitch. Surely that wasn't, there's no *way* it could be...

"Master!"

Sitting atop the cliff that served as the natural roof of the cavern sat Devlyn. Still bloated the size of a ten watermelons, his fat Imp arse spread like a cushion across the rocks of the cliff. So that's what was dislodging all those stones! The Imp's fat belly was *collapsing* the cavern!

"Quick, master!" the Imp cried. How, how in the Nine Hells had the Imp managed to get here! How had he been able to *move* when Vaskerath had commanded him, specifically commanded him to stay!

A split second after considering this, a powerful hand clamped around Vaskerath's ankle and he was pulled down from the wall. The cavern floor was strewn with leaves and the fall didn't hurt him too much. Leaves, Vaskerath thought dazedly. Dry leaves.

"Master!"

The troll left Vaskerath for the time being and turned its attention on Devlyn. Hiking his stomach up like a pair of loose trousers, the Imp lifted his fat, then let it all back down again, shattering the stone. There came a deep rumble, and then a crack like thunder as stone began to break and shift. That had been a biggie.

The troll rounded about wildly to avoid the collapsing wall. Slabs of centuries' old granite split and cracked on the ground like icicles. Violently, the chamber shook.

And through it all, Vaskerath was discovering the Path. His breathing slowed. His tiny hands knotted and unknotted, laced together, creating friction, creating flame. In the shielding cup of his hands appeared the telltale ruby. Dry leaves. There was something he could do with dry leaves.

The troll raced towards him on all fours. Vaskerath counted the seconds before they would meet, sizing up his plan, preparing. If he *had* a shot, if he wanted to save himself for anything other than a chew bone, things would need to be precise. Vaskerath counted. Five four three two...

The troll revealed its lantern mouth. Powerful yellow teeth, the crevices of which were lodged with tiny pieces of meat and bone. Vaskerath held his breath from the powerful stench, feinted nimbly, opened his palms towards the leaves and pronounced the ancient word. There was an immediate and powerful stream of flame.

The conflagration roared to life.

Twisting, spiraling, inky black smoke burst from the gnomes hands. The terrible flames rose ever higher, swallowing the troll as utterly just as the troll had been prepared to bash Vaskerath to a pulp. Matted and oily from so long a time spent in the dryness of the caverns, the troll's fur ignited at once like a torch. It flung out its arms wildly, screeching and writhing, as if it could rid itself of the fire by waving it away. But this only succeeded in spreading the conflagration further, creating a hellfire of screaming troll along the collapsing entrance.

"Devlyn!" Vaskerath found his voice. "Devlyn! I need you!"

A gust, a wind, a whip of air, and like a needle torn from a pine tree in a thunderstorm, the Imp rushed to Vaskerath's side, carving a path straight through the mounting flames. His fat body *melted* away as if it had been nothing more than water.

"We've got to go! Down there!" Vaskerath threw an arm out to indicate the passage that led off into the darkness. He hadn't been able to see it clearly before, but with the light of the fire it was now starkly illuminated.

"Whatever the master..."

"I know what I'm ordering!" Vaskerath cried, trying to make his voice heard. The shrieking troll was now fighting to get over the collapsing wall, just as Vaskerath had been trying to do just a few moments ago. "Deeper in is our only chance!"

He raised an arm and cast an illumination spell. The darkness folded back, revealing a tunnel. "Quickly!"

And even as he pronounced the last word of his spell he felt a shudder in the earth as the entrance began caving in on itself.

Vaskerath covered his head with his shirt to protect against the smoke and plunged down into the tunnel. He didn't look back. He didn't notice as the troll, clambering up the wall, blazing like a fire demon, was struck by first one mighty boulder, then another, and then a whole section of wall. He didn't pay any attention to the earth-shattering collapse that buried the troll underneath tons of boulders, sealing the entrance completely. He saw none of this. Only the pathway that led down, down, deeper and deeper, into the abyss.

Chapter 5: Spell Master

Vaskerath had known things were bad for a good long while. They had started going bad earlier that evening – had it really only been that evening and not longer? – when he began wagering his teeth, wondering if the Imp was ever going to make good on their plan to cheat the Halfling. Things had been bad at the inn when they'd been chased out and they'd only gotten worse when they'd come to the forest.

But up until this moment, Vaskerath had had a plan; even if the plan was terribly risky. It was like entrusting the concealing spell to Devlyn, when he knew right well and good that the Imp was as prepared to help him as stick a knife in his back. Or maybe his plan was to set the cave on fire. Not exactly inspired, but it'd worked.

That is, if you could say that sealing yourself up in a cave known to inhabit trolls amounted to a working plan.

Only now, in the pitch black of the caverns, his illumination was but a feeble little splotch on the mighty stalagmites foresting around them. Vaskerath felt not only lost, but truly and hopelessly defeated.

It had been hours or days, the time was the same to he and Devlyn. By his calculations, they'd probably entered into the Garom, meaning the gorge where whatever the thieves had hidden would be. Yet even the prospect of a fabulous treasure did nothing to raise Vaskerath's spirits, which had grown as dark as the surrounding blackness. He was tired, sore, demoralized, and felt beaten.

They'd wandered, fallen, stumbled, picked themselves back up, and even managed to sleep a little in these caverns, without knowing any more of where they were going aside from what could be seen from the yellow glow of Vaskerath's illumination spell. That is, up until the spell had begun to fade and he'd wisely chosen to preserve what little energy he had left for a more crucial moment in time.

As Vaskerath saw things, the particulars didn't matter much. He was going to walk until he ran out of water, then he was going to crawl, and then that would be it. Curtain closed on the life of an unfortunate, luckless, poor and trodden-down gnome, wanna be mage.

And what would happen to Devlyn? He knew what the imp thought would happen. An eternity of torment if he should die before his time. But Vaskerath knew that there existed between them a connection. He commanded and the Imp more or less fulfilled those commands. The fact that Devlyn had appeared on the roof of the cavern when Vaskerath had specifically told him to remain in the forest he had chalked up to the fact that his powers had been severely depleted, his grasp of the Path had not been one hundred percent at the time. There was a powerful connection between them, and he was beginning to wonder if Devlyn knew more than we was letting on. And it wasn't like he could simply *find out*.

Plodding along, one heavy step overtaking the other, Vaskerath turned over and fixed his eyes on the Imp, or rather, towards the direction in which he knew the Imp was located. How much did the Imp know that he'd never spoken about? How many secrets did he carry in that bald, disgusting, onion-y Imp head of his? What was Devlyn's life like before he'd been summoned?

Like most fairly knowledgeable mages, Vaskerath knew some of the basics of summoning logistics. He knew that imps, fairies and demons all came from Hel, a place no mortal had ever laid eyes on despite the fact that plenty of them had claimed to have seen it. And not just masters, but old Scribes, amateur mages and even your average drunk. Vaskerath's old master had written a book about a vision, *The Nine Tiers of Hel* or something along these lines, that he'd supposedly experienced after ingesting distilled dragon blood. As a cooked-out fairy tale, the book was wonderful. As conjurer's gospel, well... Vaskerath could stomach troll breath, but he couldn't stomach *that*.

And speaking of *smells*...

It'd been there for some time now. Certainly ever since he'd begun the dark descent down the large, spiraling pathway in the spacious central chamber of the caverns. Burnt and foul, the smell tortured his nose. But only now was Vaskerath sufficiently enraged to break the silence that had grown between him and the Imp for what felt like hours by now.

"You sloppy Imp," Vaskerath wrinkled his nose and directed a look of disgust, unfortunately lost in the darkness, towards his companion. "And I thought a little bit of rain would do you some good."

Silence. The imp implored.

"You're no fire demon," he continued. "But just a bit of a wash here and there, would that kill you? Although," he paused and said the word again, stretching it out. "*Although,* if you did die... that *is* interesting. Tell me Devlyn, what happens when imps die? Or demons for that matter? Do they go back to Hel? Can they even die? Or is there a different system? Do you know?"

Perhaps it was the exhaustion, the lack of food, too many near misses and dangers for one night, but Vaskerath was angrier than he should have been. He was angry at the situation and angry at the fact of the woken troll. And he didn't know what to do with all this excess anger *except* to direct it at the Imp, and wasn't this after all the reason why the creature was even there in the first place?

He risked a quick illumination and pivoted it towards the Imp.

Darkness was there, and nothing more.

Vaskerath spun, shining like a torch, but in every direction he was met by the same darkness.

The Imp was nowhere to be found.

How had this happened? How had he managed to lose the Imp?

Vaskerath didn't know nor did he care much about finding out. He began running down the long, natural spiraling road he'd been traveling for who knows how many leagues. And for who knew how many leagues *alone*. Hadn't the Imp been there next to him since before his illumination spell ran dry? Was his mind playing tricks on him, making him remember things that had never happened, making him experience things that didn't even exist?

The winding path was balancing out gradually. The road widened, became a disc, and broadened at the corners where enormous walls of stone swallowed up the light. The chamber was a giant tube.

And that *smell*. Burning, like some kind of burning refuse, and yet there was no light save what could be seen from the illumination streaming from his palm. Was he imagining that smell as well? Was he losing his mind in the grip of darkness and exhaustion?

Yes. It must be that, because there, in the center of the tube, Vaskerath could make out a form, as in a *human* form, draped in clothes hanging like curtains.

Not just *any* human form.

"You?" Vaskerath gasped, though he didn't know why he was even bothering to speak. The form was a construction of his mind, a memory thrown up from the past. No reality there except for what he convinced himself was real.

"Me."

The voice, the familiar baritone whisper, punctured the stillness and sent shivers down Vaskerath's spine.

No, that voice was real.

It was the Scribe.

"But you, but you're..." Vaskerath didn't know what he was trying to say. The tongue stuck in his mouth and wouldn't let the words pass. He didn't know if he was indignant or angry, or just simply surprised.

It didn't take him long to find out.

"Master!" The Imp croaked. He sat on the ground next to the Scribe. A rope was tied about his neck, and his eyes burned with fear. Vaskerath had never much liked the Imp, but seeing him trapped like this truly made him afraid.

"Shut up," the Scribe said as he jerked mercilessly at the glowing rope around the Imp's neck. Devlyn went silent.

"What do you want with him?" Vaskerath said. "Whatever else you want, if you'll let him go…"

"No, I won't be doing that," said the Scribe. "His time has come. His time and yours as well."

"What do you mean?"

"I mean precisely what I've said. His time. I am going to cut his heart out," the Scribe's voice never wavered, betrayed absolutely no expression. He might have been reading numbers. "I am going to cut his heart out," he repeated, "and sacrifice his pitiful existence to the Lord of Hel."

"Cut his heart out?" Vaskerath blinked several times. "Sacrifice?"

"You are a foolish gnome. How did you ever manage to summon an imp in the first place?"

Vaskerath did not answer. He was twisting his hands in knots, trying to work up enough energy to manage his fire spell.

The Scribe's cowl flickered, as though he was shifting his attention from one side to another. He stretched out a hand and made a gesture with the fingers that arrested Vaskerath with all the strength of an actual arm.

"Don't play with me. Answer my question," The Scribe demanded.

"I don't know," Vaskerath said, the first thing that came to mind, which just so happened to be the truth. "You can call it luck, maybe."

"Not *your* luck."

The Scribe let out a deep audible breath, as if this banter were wearisome.

"It is almost a pity," he said, seemingly as if he were speaking to himself. "Indeed, almost a pity. I do not like punishing creatures who are merely stupid. The wicked, of course, then it is justice. The stupid, this is simple cruelty."

He turned his attention back to Vaskerath. He spoke with finality. "Everything has been prepared. We've been prepared for a long time, waiting for you."

"Waiting?"

"Oh yes, many years spent waiting. You may flatter yourself if you wish, but it is true. We've wanted to get our hands on your little Imp for a long time, Vaskerath. And now it is all finished. We are prepared and you have fallen into our trap."

Vaskerath didn't like the sound of this one bit. Particularly that *we part*. Nor did he like the other noise he heard pouring up out of a dip in ground near where the Scribe was standing. The pool was shallow, and from it emanated swirling yellow smoke of foul-smelling sulfur.

"You remember, of course," the Scribe continued. "That you once tried to raise a fire demon. As little more than a novice, as far as I can recall."

"Well," Vaskerath mumbled. How in the *Nine*, how did this Scribe know that?

"And you managed an Imp instead, impressive still, for a halfwit gnome. And even more impressive is that even then you did not completely fail."

"Completely fail?"

"Yes, to raise your demon. He is here, you see, part of him, entombed in the body of this pitiful Imp. Why, haven't you ever wondered why he's been so free to disobey you? An ignorant sorcerer is no master for a demon. You've been playing with matches these five years, gnome. And now you're about to burn."

Vaskerath did not understand. Then, thunderstruck, he turned to the Imp. "You can't mean that, that Devlyn is... is a..."

But a voice interrupted him. A sibilant, snake-like voice that surely even the Scribe wasn't capable of making. *"It's time. It's timeee, Lukasssss."*

A voice from out of the pool, a voice from the *sulfur* itself came forth. A voice that made Vaskerath's skin crawl.

"Asiril will be unleashed," the Scribe murmured. "The time has come. Too long we've dealt with halfwit thieves. Too long have we suffered with that fool Davenport and these silly mages and their vain desires and their delusions of grandeur. It's time that the powerful finally seize what is rightfully theirs."

"Lukas," Vaskerath ran the name over his tongue. "Lukas."

"Master," Devlyn whimpered. "Save me!"

"It's *timmmmmmme. Killllllll the Imp.*"

The Scribe sighed and drew off his cowl. Vaskerath knew that face, a man from his memory, from his youth, from his early days as a mage, from when he was learning his first incantations. But how?

"Spellmaster Lukas?"

The Master raised his arms and murmured an incantation. An icy sensation like claws gripped Vaskerath's head. He bellowed in agony, and then knew no more.

The Imp, Devlyn, looked at Vaskerath, withering in pain. The Imp could feel the thong tighten around his neck as he was pulled by the Master towards the pool.

The painful, icy coldness continued to engulf Vaskerath's head and body. His two hands where somehow behind his back and they were rubbing each other even without Vaskerath's doing. His hands of their own accord seemed trying to bring back at least a small fire spell to break the Master's hold. It was useless; he couldn't say the words he needed.

Gnome and Imp's eyes met. "The Imp is part Fire Demon," Vaskerath thought. It didn't seem possible, but...

Devlyn looked from Vaskerath to the Scribe and back. The Fire Demon inside of him longed for freedom. It was that part of him that allowed the Imp his occasional forays into freedom without the gnome. The fire demon knew that if the gnome died, a more terrible fate awaited it.

Vaskerath could feel his ties to Devlyn in the sulfur pool. This wasn't about being bound to a more powerful master. This was about bringing Devlyn's alter ego, Asiril, the Lord of Fire Demons to this world.

Devlyn's neck began to burn with rage. The Imp's eyes locked on Vaskerath. The gnome felt the heat begin to grow in his hands.

"With me, Master," the Imp cried out.

An explosion of white light and fire engulfed them, gnome, Imp and Scribe. The Scibe's eye were blinded by the light. The heat roared over them and was gone, and so were Vaskerath and his Imp.

"What? How did you do that gnome?" The Scribe screamed. He had underestimated the gnome's abilities. That wouldn't happen again.

Vaskerath had closed his eyes to the flash of light and the heat. He had somehow, with Devlyn's help, cast the spell that had freed them. He was standing outside of the caverns, free under the star lit sky. In the distance stood Garom's Gorge. His Imp, Devlyn, stood at his side.

"We are free... Master?" the Imp asked Vaskerath.

Vaskerath looked at the Imp. Somehow, they were far from the mountain. Had he done this? It couldn't have been the Imp alone. Somehow, together, they had cast an impossible spell. Their connection together now seemed stronger than ever, and that made Vaskerath shudder involuntarily.

"Follow me, Imp," Vaskerath commanded as he started to walk, the Scribes purse now clutched in his right hand.

The End of Book 1

<u>Sneak Preview of The Angel's Blessing</u>

Chapter 1 The Day of the White Rook

My Master did not become the great Warrior Shaman of peace because he was born with the blessings of the gods. He did not rise to his exalted place in the history of our worlds by the chance of ancestry, nor was he a child of fortune. He had no advantage other than his cunning, and he had no blessing other than that given to him by his grandfather. And that blessing was herb-lore.

My master was conceived and born in violence.

His mother was a young beauty who was ravaged by the invading Veylus pirates when our beloved city of Barnacle Atoll was overrun. When her time to give birth came, she held the newborn infant to her breast, the scrawny infant seeking to suckle a tit. But the nipple that the child found was cold and so he turned to his grandfather's thumb instead, and that thumb was hard and calloused and yet rich with the taste of mother-earth and her herbs. And so in his first suckle of life, the babe that was to be known simply as Kell, tasted the roots of us all.

Kell spent his youngest years under the domination of the brigands, and he quickly learned stealth and cunning as a way of life. In time, the Veylus were ousted by the armada of Queen Anastasias, and while her liberation was near devastation, the people of the Barnacles were once again free. With that freedom came years of reconstruction and tribute to the Queen, but that was far better than the pirates.

In that time Kell grew up as boys will. He was astounded with the world. His grandfather had a bountiful garden, and in there Kell saw crawlers and wigglers and flyers of all sorts. As a toddler, he tasted them and found them much crunchier than the wiggly ones of the root cellar. His grandfather often looked at him and sighed as adults will. But despite his odd tastes, he grew up healthy and strong.

Their small island of Dunsil wasn't on many sea-routes, but he and his grandfather were often visited by passing ships looking for a remedy to help a wounded or sick crewman. Often a boatful of sailors would come ashore and seek one of grandfather's special elixirs, and then ask of the ways with which to work the earth's gift. His grandfather never refused anyone in need -- for a fair price. Over the years, the legends grew of his incredible remedies. It was an ideal childhood and Kell was very happy.

Until the day that the Dorimans engulfed their island.

They were a gang of thugs with ships. Their fleet was small and fast and they would prey on defenseless lands, not to conquer, but to plunder and destroy. And before the Queen's forces could come to aid, they would sail away into the night's fog only to reappear in some other land, rough-handed and demanding. They wore no uniforms, and in their motley gear Kell saw them as something to be afraid of. He was a teenager at the time and the Dorimans saw him as a value to their number. And so at his grandfather's urging, he drew on all his cunning and he ran away.

He ran across the crest of the island and to the common ground where others were also gathering and afraid. Understanding his plight, the elders brought him to a cove with a light boat hidden within. They told him to sail straight to Angove's Cay, which was the home of Wendfala the Witch.

The young witch, seeing my Master's comely and youthful state, took him in and proceeded to teach him the ancient ways. It is said that in those dark hours while our very island writhed beneath the boots of the Dorimans, Wendfala made my Master into a man, and the young boy emerged from her clutches alert, able and with a new sort of strength that radiated off him like an aura.

They say that he emerged from her embraces as a magical paladin who single-handedly rallied the people and sent the Dorimans howling away and afraid. They say that he was the hero who liberated our islands and that the Doriman still fear his name. And they say that when he was done with the Dorimans, the of battle was still upon him, and so he sailed the world in search of glory, wisdom and to inflict Holy Justice upon the wicked. For years sailors and merchants would land on our island and tell tales of Kell's valor in lands unknown.

That's what they say.

In the years of peace that followed many tales were told and retold, and then told and changed again and again. And in the small confines of the island of Dunsil the simple herbalist's grandchild became a living legend.

He returned to our island the year that I was born, and while many looked at the legendary hero in awe, their real amazement was that the lad looked as if he had never left. It was as though time had not touched him, and when he walked into his grandfather's cottage with his backpack full of magic and treasures, the old man simply looked up and told him that the garden needed tending.

He would say nothing of his adventures, but people would talk. Kell shunned their stories, but he didn't shun their company. He was still young and he had a quick wit at the tavern and loved winning at darts and skittles. The young women all eyed him and so at the festivals and dances he never lacked a partner. His knowledge of herbs and medicines grew as his grandfather taught him all he knew as he waned in years. People came to trust the young man as they did his old grandfather, sometimes more.

In time, the great herbalist finally passed. Every man woman and child on Dunsil stood on the white sands of the island's eastern shore as Kell made ready the last boat. They covered his body in beautiful flower blossoms, in hopes that the sea would pause and delight in the scent and so allow fair winds to carry him to his eternal paradise. Even the witch Wendfala came to give her blessing.

I was just a small boy at the time. I remember my mother urging me, my sisters and my brothers to let go of our flowers. But I was fascinated by the naked old man. He was nothing but old bones wrapped in tan skin at the bottom of a small rustic boat, and yet the blossoms made him seem almost alive.

"Forgive my child Kell," my mother said. "He is –"

"Young," Kell said. "And fascinated."

Then he set his gaze on me and he smiled.

It was not that long after the funeral that I was selected to be Kell's apprentice. I trembled with the honor and surged with excitement.

I had heard all of the grand tales. Indeed, I had been raised in the shadow of those magnificent stories, and when he and my father bartered for my apprenticeship, I thought that the gods themselves had blessed me.

"He's kind of scrawny."

"Yeah," my father said. "He is. But how much bulk do you need to scratch out your herbs?"

Kell frowned.

"Look," my father said. "I have a farm. Farming is a strong man's job. The boy will be better in your hands. I will give you milk, cheese and all the whey you want for four years."

"Seven."

I listened as they haggled over my worth. In the end I went for the price of six years of milk, three of cheeses and all the whey I could carry between the houses until I was seventeen.

It was a good bargain.

Master Kell was a soft-spoken and kindly man. He treated me well and our house wanted for nothing. Along with teaching me herb lore, he also taught me numbers and letters, and while I found numbers valuable in weighing and mixing and figuring out the price to put on a remedy, I never understood why Kell put so much value on writing.

We worked in a daily routine and there were always things to get done or learn. But Kell was a light-hearted soul and we often took the time to play. We would sometimes end a long day frolicking and fishing on one side of Crystal Lake while the women washed their laundry on the other. My master had an eye for the ladies and there were quite a few nights that I spent alone sleeping under the Starlight.

When I came into my teenage years I learned two very important lessons of life. One was girls. When I was young girls were simply giggly playmates, but as I matured I began to see those gigglers grow round, soft and firm, and that made me wonder. And there were odd things about my own body that I didn't understand; strange stirrings and desires. I asked my master about these feelings but he seemed somewhat at a loss, then smiled and assured me that all would be revealed in time.

I wondered about how long that time might be. And then one day a woman named Loleena came calling. She was from the other side of the island and I barely knew her. Kell graciously invited her to sup with us and the woman seemed to take an immediate interest in me. I was flattered that such a fine lady would even recognize my existence, let along talk with me.

The night was cool and getting cooler. Kell excused himself to gather more wood for the fire, but he didn't return till dawn. And that night Loleena helped me understand what it was like to be a man.

Over time I became an expert at herb lore and my master's special elixirs where in high demand, giving me plenty of practice at the craft. When it came time for the harvest festival, I was invited for the first time to join the adults around the big bonfire. There was music and dancing, and everyone cheered when Kell produced a keg of his special brew. The draught was sweet and heady and at first I didn't feel its effects. But then the festival started to feel a lot more happier to me. The dancing was lighter, the music was sweeter, and the young girls seemed prettier. The brew seemed to have the same effect on the girls as well, because they suddenly found me handsome. I did not lack for sweet company all that day and night.

Winters on the Atoll were usually cold and dreary. Work still needed to be done, but the sun would set earlier and earlier and the nights cooped up in the cottage could be wearisome. In those days I was glad to have learned my letters. My master had books on his craft and a boring volume entitled *The List of Leaves* that helped pass the dreary time.

We woke one chill sunny morning to a racket outside. Rooks were calling and crying. We rushed outside to see what was happening and the sky was nearly blotted out by their numbers. It was an amazing sight. Thousands of them were circling overhead. They seemed to be whirling in a vortex that narrowed closer and closer to the center eye, and in that eye I saw a single speck of white.

As we watched the birds became more and more frantic. The center mass of birds began to dip down and then formed into a funnel. I cried out and fell back to shield myself, but when they were only a few hundred feet above us a single rook parted from the myriad, spread its massive wings and began to descend. As it got closer we could see that the rook was as white as snow.

The pearlescent feathers seemed almost to gleam and its beak was like polished marble, but even as its spiny claws touched the sand of the earth the creature transformed. There stood before us a tall, bald man with skin as black as the night that seemed to almost shine blue where the sunlight fell on it. He was hairless from his head to his eyebrows and everywhere else a man should have hair. But what truly astonished me was that there was no manhood. At the place where his thighs met his pelvis there was nothing but smooth dark flesh.

"You are Kell," the man said in a silky, almost liquid voice.

"I am."

And for all of my amazement and growing fear my master was as calm as the sea on a spring morning.

"I am an emissary from Wendfala," he said. "The Witch calls on your pledge."

There was a long pause before my master spoke. The birds above had wheeled out in a huge circle letting the sun shine onto us.

"Why doesn't Wendfala come herself to call on this sacred pledge?" Kell asked in a powerful voice.

"She has been kidnapped," the man-bird said.

"Kidnapped?" Kell bellowed, his hand unconsciously flexing as if to grab his weapon.

"She needs your help. In fact the whole of the Nine domains need your help."

"With what? What is going on?" Kell asked with obvious concern in his voice.

"Wendfala calls for you. It's not for me to judge her choice. I am only a messenger and ask you to hear her plea. I see smoke from your chimney. Can we go inside? It's cold out here without feathers."

"Um, sure. But first tell me, what is your name?" said Kell

"I am Byrinius."

Kell motioned towards his house and as they turned to go inside Byrinius pointed towards me and asked who I was.

"This is Longo Nonan," Kell said. "He is my apprentice."

"Longo," the man said. "Look at me boy. I have no hair and I have nothing where a human male should have something. But can you tell me what else there is about me that is not like you?"

At first I was frightened and my brain refused to work. But it felt as though the two would stare at me until I either flushed or fumbled like a child, or I solved the riddle. I looked. Then I looked again, and then I saw, but the words would not form and so I simply pointed to my belly.

"That's right," Byrinius said laughing long and hard. "I have no naval. I was not born, I was hatched. Kell, the lad is astute. Let him come with us and listen."

My master gave me a strange look, but I went with them and sat quietly in the corner. Kell offered tea but the man refused. He plucked a large ember from the fire, sat at the table, and held the glowing thing in his palm as he spoke.

"Visalth is coming," the man said.

As he spoke, vapors rose from the glowing ember. The smoke grew a little and then began to spin, then gather and spread into a wide sphere, and in the center of the sphere an image began to form. It was the image of a giant skeletal Dragon... A Bone Dragon.

I had heard of such things in stories, and in my youth they were terrifying. The mindless, soulless things would always seek to steal, kill and destroy and they could listen to no reason and had no fear for their own lives.

But these were modern times. Such myths were put away long ago along with frost fairies and trolls.

But that day my eyes had seen a bird transform into the vestige of a man who was now holding a scorching cinder in his hand as if it were a pebble, and the vision that formed in the room made me believe.

The dragon's bones were not like the white bleached things of men I had seen washed up on the beaches. They were deep brown like rotten teeth. It's long skull was swept back, flaring out into nine horns that turned forward like barbed fish-hooks. The hollow orbits were long, narrow and without eyes. It had a look of evil about it. I could not count the many spike-tipped vertebrae of the creature's neck, but the thing could wind and twist like a snake. Its ribs were slender, but what once had been the torso was long. Its fore-limbs grew from a solid breast-plate that looked scarred and beaten, and they were like a man's arms ending in grasping fingers. Its massive hind-legs bent like a deer, but the thighs could have been as thick as a trader ship's mast, and the claws could have crushed our house. The wings that sprouted from its back spread like enormous bird fingers, but between those bones there was no skin, only what looked like remnants of tattered sails or the clinging bits of flesh from creatures undreamed. The tail of the beast was easily as long as the whole creature, and as I watched the dragon fly about in the vision, the bony tail would whip back between the wings to attack like a scorpion.

"Magnificent," Kell said. "Truly a feat of powerful magic."

"Dark magic," Byrinius replied.

We watched the scene as the dragon lay waste to a solid castle set on a hill. The land was unknown to me. It was a lush place with rolling green grass, well cultivated farm land surrounded by walls and then a deep forest. But as we watched, the beast seemed to delight in wreaking ruin on the castle walls and buildings. An army of warriors looked helpless against the skeletal foe. Their arrows and bolts would bounce off the bones or sail through the empty spaces of its ribs. Even the catapults the men managed to muster had little effect, and they were quickly destroyed. When the undead horror had reduced the defenses to rubble it then turned on the army, sweeping men and cavalry away with its deadly tail.

"It seems bent on wanton destruction," Kell said.

"Not so. There is method in its madness. Observe."

I watched with a dull growing terror. When the army had been broken and the warriors were fleeing, men began to march in from the woods. The dragon seemed to suddenly heed some sort of call. It lifted and flew up on wings that were no wings, circling the walled city as the invaders easily took over.

"What are we seeing?" Kell asked. "What place is this?"

"It's Breakstone Hold, the Castle of Duke Venyez in Estile."

"Estile? That's in the Nine."

"It is," the man said. "It is on the Queen's western realms. The bone dragon's name is Visalth, and it's forces seem to be working their way along the alliance. Before Estile, the Duchy of Halnn fell. But the curious thing about the invasion is the pattern of assault. There is no warning, but just before an invasion all magic seems to disappear."

"What?"

"Wizards," the man went on, "witches, mages, even holy paladins seem to disappear. Whether these are physical or spiritual abductions I cannot say. But I do know that when Visalth appears there are none who can stand before him – they all disappear or get destroyed. And now Wendfala is captured, and from her prison she sends me to you ahead of the storm to get your aid."

Kell gulped his tea. The mystical scene vanished but Byrinius still held the glowing ember. My master stood and paced the room. He ran his fingers through his hair again and again. Then he finally stood before the window and gazed out to sea. He stood a long time. He then seemed decisive and strode to a locked wardrobe. He held his fingers over the handle and mumbled a quick verse. The doors popped open and from the inside he drew out a long and stout war-hammer that was glowing brightly.

The weapon was easily as long as my arm. Its handle was wrapped with red leather that showed stains of wear and sweat. The oaken shaft was carved in a hexagon. Cold blue steel ran from the crown down that shaft and was bolted with iron. The broad, flat head could easily have crushed an Ogres Skull, and the opposite side of the hammer was a nasty six sided piece of magical steel ending in a sharp point. The pommel was thick and ended with an 8 inch long double-bladed knife made of Admantium with a magically sharpened blade. Kell tossed his trusty weapon onto the table and the weight of it shook the table and dented it in several places.

"This is my little friend Ashrune," my master said. "How might we help?"

"You need to Flee this place." Byrinius said in a grave and urgent tone.

"Never! I will not run when my Queen's lands are in danger. I am no coward." Kell bellowed, outrage in his voice.

"Bravery in the face of such a monster is suicide," Byrinius said calmly. "The power behind Visalth is cunning, and so you must be just as crafty. Ashrune may be a noble weapon but even with the might of a Titan behind, it would barely scratch the creature's skull before you were impaled. You need something far mightier, and to find such a thing you need help that is beyond simple magic. You need an Angel."

Check out the rest of the story in book or audio book format on my website: www.LordHartRules.com

My Other Books and Audio Books

THE ANGEL'S BLESSING
HOLY PALADIN'S QUEST
BLAINE HART

SPELL MASTER
WIZARD'S QUEST
BLAINE HART

Blaine Hart
The Bard's Tale
A Mysterious Journey

THE SANDS OF TIME
THE ANGEL'S BLESSING
BLAINE HART

For A Special Treat, check out my
<u>AUDIO BOOKS</u>

Thanks for reading!

If you enjoyed this book a nice review would be greatly appreciated.

Check Out all My Books and Audio Books at:
www.LordHartRules.com